'WELL-LOVED TALES'

The Princess and the Pea

A LADYBIRD 'EASY-READING' BOOK

retold by
VERA SOUTHGATE, M.A., B.Com.

with illustrations by
ERIC WINTER

Publishers: Wills & Hepworth Ltd., Loughborough

First published 1967   ©   Printed in England

THE PRINCESS AND THE PEA

Once upon a time, there was a prince. When he grew up he wanted to marry a princess. But he wanted her to be a *real* princess.

0 7214 0085 X

Series 606D

The prince went all over the world looking for a *real* princess whom he could marry.

The prince met many princesses but there was always something the matter with them. One was too tall and another was too small. One was too sad and another was too gay.

Somehow or other, not one of the princesses was just right. The prince was never quite sure if they were *real* princesses.

At last, the prince came home again. He was very sad because he did want to marry a *real* princess.

Then one night there was a terrible storm. The lightning flashed, the thunder roared, the wind blew and the rain poured down.

In the middle of the storm there was a knock on the door of the castle. The old king went to open the door.

There, standing outside in the pouring rain, was a lovely lady. She might have been a princess, but she was so wet that it was difficult to tell.

Her hair was so wet that the water from it was running down her face. Her clothes were so wet that the water was pouring out of them. Her shoes were so wet that the water was running in at the toes and out at the heels.

The king led the princess into the castle, out of the wind and the rain.

There she stood, in a pool of water, and all she could say was, " I am a *real* princess."

The prince could not believe his ears when he heard her say, "I am a *real* princess."

The old queen heard her say, "I am a *real* princess."

"We'll see about that," thought the old queen, but she did not say anything.

While the princess was being bathed and dried and dressed in dry clothes, the queen went to see about a bedroom for her.

The queen had all the bedclothes taken off the bed. Then she put a pea under the mattress.

Then more mattresses were put on top, until there were twenty mattresses on top of the pea.

Then the queen had twenty feather beds piled on top of the twenty mattresses.

"Now we shall find out if you are a real princess," said the queen to herself.

When the princess was warmed and fed, the queen led her to the bedroom and tucked her into bed.

In the morning, the old queen went to see the princess. "How did you sleep, my dear?" she asked her.

"Dreadfully," replied the princess, "I hardly slept a wink all night!"

"What was the matter?" asked the old queen.

"I do not know what was in the bed," replied the princess, "but there was something hard in it. Now I am black and blue all over."

Then the queen knew that this was a *real* princess because she had felt the pea through twenty mattresses and twenty feather beds. Only a *real* princess could be as tender as that.

The prince was filled with joy when the old queen told him that they had indeed found a *real* princess.

Now the queen had the pea taken out of the bed so that the poor princess could sleep well.

A wedding was arranged between the prince and the *real* princess. Then there was great joy in the castle.

As for the pea, it was placed in a museum. It may still be seen there—if no-one has taken it away!